Disney

It's a Small World

I LOVE SCHOOL!

Written by Calliope Glass
Illustrated by Caroline LaVelle Egan and Winnie Ho

Printed in the United States of America
First Edition   1 3 5 7 9 10 8 6 4 2
J689-1817-1-12122
Library of Congress Catalog Card Number: 2012933311
ISBN 978-1-4231-6231-5
For more Disney Press fun, visit www.disneybooks.com

Disney PRESS

New York

It's Monday morning—time to go to school! In the **United States**, **Andrew** takes the school bus.

In **China**, **Ling's** father walks her to school on his way to work.

In **Italy**, **Dario** rides his bicycle to school.
He's looking forward to seeing his friends.

SCUOLA ➡

In **South Africa**, Zanele's mother and father kiss her good-bye for the day.

At **Dario's** school, the students are learning to tell time. The clock has an hour hand and a minute hand. **"Who knows what time it is?"** the teacher asks. **Dario** raises his hand. **"It's nine o'clock!"** he says.

It's time for music class at **Zanele's** school. The students are learning to play African drums.

Bom!

Bom! Bom!

Zanele loves the deep
sound of her drum.

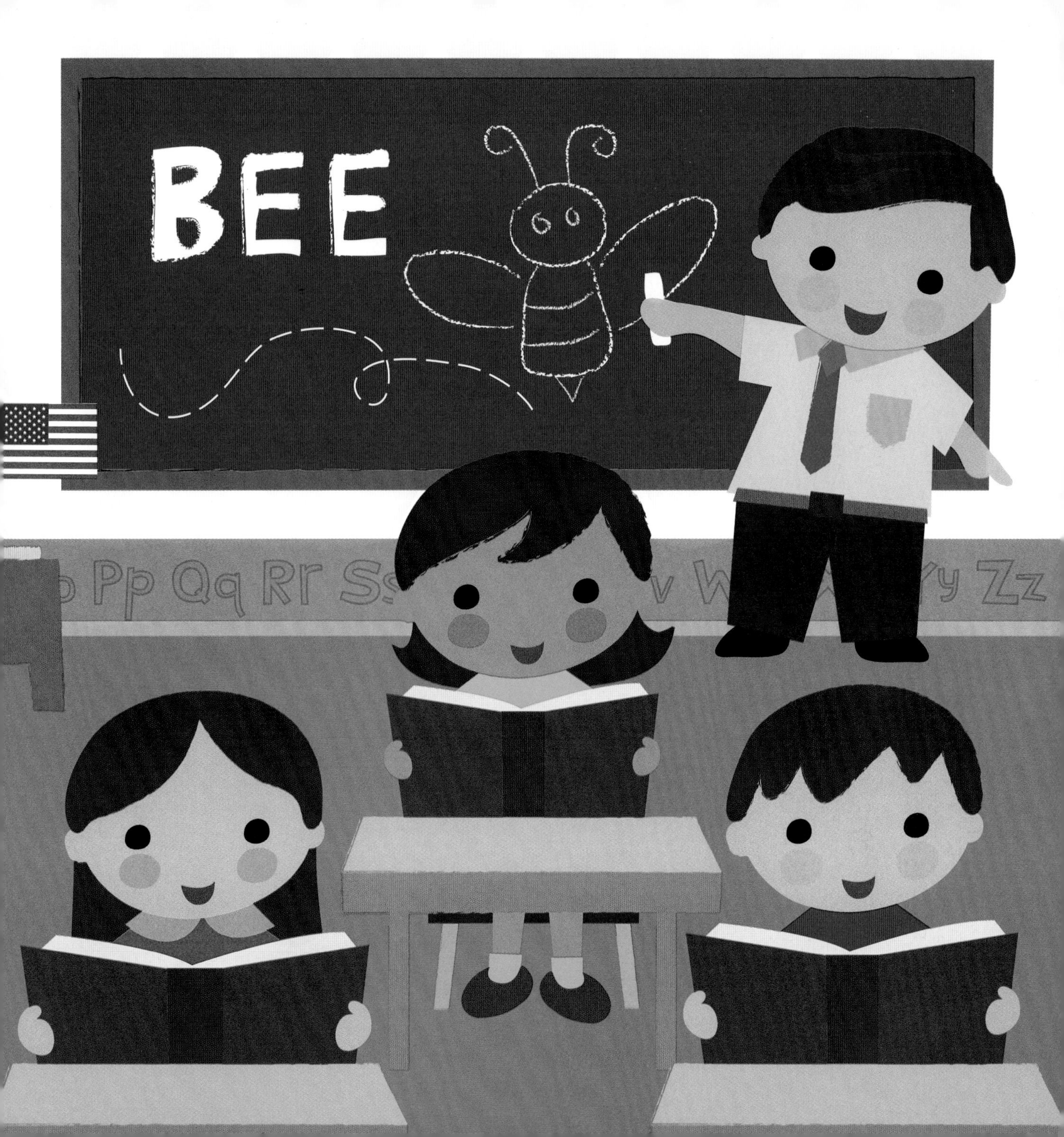
BEE

热爱祖国

"China is a very old country," Ling's teacher says. Her class is studying Chinese history. One thousand years ago, China was ruled by an emperor. Ling has a picture of him. She thinks his hat makes him look very wise.

Soon it's lunchtime! In **Italy**, **Dario** and his friends eat pasta with tomato sauce.

In **South Africa**, **Zanele** eats corn porridge and vegetable stew.

Andrew and his classmates in the United States eat turkey sandwiches.

In China, Ling eats rice with vegetables and tofu.

At recess, **Ling** and her classmates play Catch the Dragon's Tail. They line up.

Ling is at the front. She is the dragon's head.
Can she tag the tail while everyone stays in line?

Math is **Zanele's** favorite subject. She uses seashells to practice addition. The class collected the shells on a trip to the seashore.

"**Two plus three is five**," says **Zanele**.

"**Three plus two is five**," says **Zanele's** friend.

"You're both right!" says the teacher.

In the afternoon, Dario and his friends have gym class. They choose teams for soccer. In **Italy** they call it *calcio.* They try to see who will get a goal first.

Zanele draws a lion in art class. Her friend draws
a giraffe. They use crayons on smooth white paper.

Zanele imagines her lion chasing the giraffe. She draws
lines behind the lion. Now it looks like it's running.

Andrew's class has a pet. His name is Fernando, and he is a turtle.

"**Fernando hatched from an egg,**" Andrew's friend Katie says just before the bell rings. The class is studying animals. They learned that turtles lay eggs, just like chickens.

At the end of the day,
it's **time to go home.**

SCHOOL BUS

But tomorrow everyone
will be back for another
fun day at **school.**